Please return/renew this item by the
last date shown to avoid a charge.
Books may also be renewed by phone
and Internet. May not be renewed if
required by another reader.
www.libraries.barnet.gov.uk

LONDON BOROUGH

D1440487

LONDON ⌐⌐⌐ OF BARNET

'Big Foot'
An original concept by Heather Pindar
© Heather Pindar

Illustrated by Natalie Briscoe

Published by MAVERICK ARTS PUBLISHING LTD

Studio 11, City Business Centre, 6 Brighton Road,

Horsham, West Sussex, RH13 5BB

© Maverick Arts Publishing Limited November 2020

+44 (0)1403 256941

A CIP catalogue record for this book is available at the British Library.

ISBN 978-1-84886-716-1

www.maverickbooks.co.uk

Gold

This book is rated as: Gold Band (Guided Reading)

Big Foot

By **Heather Pindar**

Illustrated by
Natalie Briscoe

Chapter 1

Danni looked at her fluffy orange onesie. It was a birthday present from her Aunt Jess.

The dark orange fur made Danni think of tigers, bears and wild monsters.

That gave her an idea. She could pretend to be a monster! It would be the perfect trick to play on her best friend, Sameer.

Danni looked in the garden shed for more costume ideas.

She found two old tennis rackets and a broken chair. She broke off some thin pieces of wood from the chair and nailed them to the edges of the tennis rackets.
They looked just like claws.

Danni climbed into her orange onesie.
Then she strapped the rackets to her feet
using two old belts.

Her monster outfit was ready.

Chapter 2

Danni knew Sameer would be walking through the woods at five thirty. It was a short cut to his Judo class.

At five o'clock, Danni put the tennis racket feet under her arm and sneaked out of her garden gate.

She walked into the woods and then put on her monster feet.

Slowly, Danni jumped along the main path through the woods. She looked back and saw she had made a trail of neat footprints. They were large and deep.

Danni took off her monster feet and hid them under a pile of leaves. Then she crouched down and waited.

At last she saw Sameer in the distance. He was practising his Judo kicks and jumps as he came down the path. Danni saw Sameer stop suddenly. It was where she had been walking in her monster shoes.

Danni watched him bend down to look more closely at the ground.

'NOW!' thought Danni.

She leapt out of the hedge and ran along the edge of the field.

She checked to make sure Sameer had seen her. Then she hid in some bushes.

Sameer left the path and ran across the field, looking all around him.

A little girl and her mum were there too, but none of them spotted Danni hiding in the bushes.

'They fell for my trick,' thought Danni.
As soon as Sameer and the others had gone,
she ran home, giggling all the way.
Danni couldn't wait to see Sameer at school
the next day.

Chapter 3

"You'll never guess what I saw!" Sameer began. "I was on my way to Judo and I saw these footprints in the mud. Not people's footprints. They were great big MONSTER FOOTPRINTS!"

Danni tried to look amazed. "Go on!" she said.

"And then I saw it," said Sameer.

"I saw this orange hairy thing running across the field! It looked a bit like a bear. Or maybe more like a tiger. This girl was there too with her mum. They took some photos. We were all just... AMAZED."

"Wow!" said Danni. "I've got something amazing to tell you as well. Meet me after school. You won't believe your eyes."

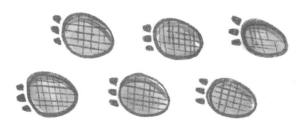

Chapter 4

Sameer put on Danni's wild monster feet.

He tried making some monster footprints.

"So it was you, Danni! That's so clever. I wish I'd thought of it first!"

He pulled out his phone. "Have you seen this?" He scrolled through to the news for their town.

'Big Foot Monster seen in woods. Huge footprints found!' it said. And just above was a photo of something orange and hairy running across a field.

"Big Foot. That's a brilliant name!" said Sameer. "You've got to keep on being Big Foot."

"Alright," giggled Danni. "I will."

It was easier for Danni to play the part of Big Foot now she had Sameer to help her. He showed her how to use face paints to make her Big Foot outfit look even better.

It was fun to hide in the woods and jump out at people. She loved to see people looking at the Big Foot prints in the mud too.

At first, the Big Foot story made people in the town a little bit nervous. But soon they started to enjoy the mystery.

More and more people went for walks in the woods to try and see Big Foot. They began to use Big Foot as an excuse – if something went missing or got broken they would say: 'It wasn't me. Big Foot must have done it'.

The shops started selling Big Foot mugs, tea towels, key rings, giant hairy orange slippers and orange cuddly monster toys.

But then things started to go wrong.
Lots of newspapers and TV shows started
reporting the Big Foot story. Hundreds of
Big Foot fans arrived in cars and buses.

The streets were crowded. The bins spilled
over. The hills and woods near Danni's house
became noisy. The deer, birds and other wild
animals were scared away.

Some people even made a trap in the woods
to catch Big Foot.

The mayor told everyone she wanted to build
a 'Big Foot' shopping centre and car park.
It would be built in the woods near Danni's
house.

Chapter 5

"I don't like it," said Danni to Sameer.

They were walking to a new part of the woods to make some footprints. Sameer was carrying the Big Foot monster feet in his backpack. Danni was wearing her Big Foot outfit. "I don't like all this noise and rubbish, and the animals being scared away. The shopping centre will make things much worse. I'm going to stop being Big Foot."

"Don't give up being Big Foot," said Sameer. "Big Foot is so much fun! Everyone will be sad and bored without Big Foot."

Danni marched ahead of Sameer on the narrow path. Suddenly she spun upwards. She screamed. An alarm started bleeping. Danni was caught in a net.

"It's the Big Foot trap!" said Sameer.

Some people ran up the path.

"Big Foot's in the trap!" they shouted. They started taking photos.

"Stop!" said Sameer. "Look how scared Big Foot is! It's not fair." He leapt up and pulled the net down. He quickly let Danni out of the net. She ran away at top speed.

Chapter 6

The photos of Big Foot, looking scared in the net, went in the town's newspaper. Everyone felt sorry for Big Foot.

Danni and Sameer wrote a letter to the newspaper. The letter said the shopping centre and car park would ruin the woods and frighten away the animals. Why not have a Big Foot nature park instead? People could have fun without leaving rubbish or scaring the animals.

DAILY NEWS

BIGFOOT
SCARED?

Hundreds of people wrote to the mayor saying they agreed with Sameer and Danni.

The mayor said 'yes' to the nature park.

The builders and gardeners began work on the new park soon afterwards. They built it on some land near the town that no one used anymore.

The Big Foot Nature Park became a wild and wonderful place for lots of animals, including humans and Big Foot monsters.

Danni sometimes went there as Big Foot, just for fun. Sometimes she went as herself with her friends. Sometimes she saw other children dressed in their own Big Foot costumes.

The sign at the gate said: "**BIG FOOT NATURE PARK. LEAVE ONLY FOOTPRINTS, BIG OR SMALL...**"

The End

Book Bands for Guided Reading

The Institute of Education book banding system is a scale of colours that reflects the various levels of reading difficulty. The bands are assigned by taking into account the content, the language style, the layout and phonics. Word, phrase and sentence level work is also taken into consideration.

Maverick Early Readers are a bright, attractive range of books covering the pink to white bands. All of these books have been book banded for guided reading to the industry standard and edited by a leading educational consultant.

To view the whole Maverick Readers scheme, visit our website at
www.maverickearlyreaders.com

Or scan the QR code above to view our scheme instantly!

Pink
Red
Yellow
Blue
Green
Orange
Turquoise
Purple
Gold
White